MOISHE'S MIRACLE

A HANUKKAH STORY

By Laura Krauss Melmed

Illustrated by David Slonim

chronicle books · san francisco

Starlight, star bright

Magic on a winter's night

White snow, candle glow

Far away and long ago . . .

In the poor village of Wishniak lived a milkman named Moishe and his wife, Baila. Since he owned only two cows, Moishe earned a meager living. Still, he was known as a generous man, always ready to help his neighbors. Baila scrubbed and cooked and tried to scrape together a few kopeks for a nice Sabbath meal. But oy! How she could scold! Everyone said she had the sharpest tongue in Wishniak and little patience for Moishe's generous ways.

It was early winter, and already the wind prowled the icy lanes of the village like a starving jackal. Many were feeling the pangs of hunger—Malka the widow and her ailing son Shmuel; Heshy Fenster, out of work, with his wife expecting their thirteenth child; frail Bubby Rifka, housebound with her calico cat. Moishe left an extra quart of milk here, a pint of thick cream there.

On the night before the holiday of Hanukkah was to begin, Baila untied her *knippel*, the knot in her handkerchief in which she kept their money, and shook the handkerchief in Moishe's face. "Empty! All because of your foolish generosity. How will I buy the eggs and flour to make our Hanukkah latkes, much less the oil to fry them in?"

Moishe imagined coins falling from the handkerchief into Baila's pan, where they turned into golden potato pancakes. He could almost smell those latkes frying!

Oh well, he thought with a sigh, we ought to be thankful for what we have.

"Bailaleh, don't fret," he soothed. "There are enough onions and potatoes for a nice pot of soup."

But Baila would not listen. "How did I end up with this *schlemiel* when I could have married the baker's son?" On and on she scolded, hands on her hips and eyes rolled heavenward, until Moishe fled to the cowshed for some peace.

He flopped down in the straw. How sleepy he felt . . .

"MOO-oishe! MOO-oishe!" The milkman sat up suddenly. Rubbing his eyes, he looked around to see who was calling him. Imagine his astonishment when he found that it was one of his cows!

"You have always cared well for us, Moishe. You keep our shed clean, milk us on time, and feed us plenty."

"MOO-ost assuredly," chimed in the other cow. "So, although we seldom reveal to humans our power to speak, we want to help you, dear Moishe."

"While you were sleeping here tonight," the first cow went on, "a stranger came to the shed. For hours he entertained us with tales of magic and adventure. You snored loudly all the while! But before leaving, he hid a gift for you, there, under the straw." She pointed with her velvety black nose.

"For me?" Moishe reached down and felt something cold and hard. He pulled out a battered frying pan encrusted with grease. "An old pan?" He tried not to show his disappointment.

"But such a pan!" exclaimed the second cow. "According to the stranger, you have only to set it upon the fire totally empty, and it will produce as many delicious Hanukkah latkes as you wish. Latkes by the dozens, latkes by the hundreds will appear until you remove the pan from the stove. Just remember the stranger's warning: 'To Moishe this gift was given, and *only Moishe must use it.*'"

Moishe was overjoyed. He showered thanks on the cows and milked them, for it was early morning. Then he returned to the house and hid the frying pan on top of the wardrobe, intending to surprise his wife with it later on.

That evening Moishe and Baila lit the first Hanukkah candle with the *shammes*, the candle used to light the others. They would add a candle to the menorah on each of the eight nights of Hanukkah. With the menorah glowing in the window, Moishe took down the magic frying pan and told Baila all that had happened in the cowshed, being careful to repeat the stranger's warning. Of course, Baila believed not a word of Moishe's story. "I've never heard anything so *meshugah* in all my life!" she scoffed. "A pan is a pan."

Nevertheless, Moishe placed the pan over the fire. A lively sizzle filled the air. Soon the rich aroma of potatoes and onions frying made Moishe's nose twitch and Baila's mouth water. And then there were latkes—plump as little pillows, with edges like golden lace.

The latkes were so light, they floated right into the air as they finished cooking! Baila and Moishe leaped about the kitchen, catching them. When each had a plateful, Moishe removed the pan from the fire. Then he and Baila ate their fill and went to bed.

How Moishe tossed and turned that night, twisting the coverlet into knots! Perhaps he had eaten too many latkes. In his dreams he saw Shmuel and Bubby Rifka, the calico cat and the Fenster brood. They marched around his bed holding empty plates and staring at him with hungry eyes.

The next morning Moishe left a note on every doorstep: *Happy Hanukkah! Please come for latkes tonight at Moishe the milkman's!*

It seemed that all of Wishniak squeezed into Moishe and Baila's little house that night. Latkes galore sailed from the magic pan. There was singing and dancing to Heshy's accordion, and the children spun *dreidels*, little Hanukkah tops. Only Baila stood apart, shaking her head. Moishe was giving things away, as usual, and making a mess of her house. If she could just get rid of him for a while, she would take matters into her own hands.

The next day, Baila hid the Hanukkah candles under the bed.

"Moishe, there are six more days of Hanukkah left, and all our candles are gone," she wailed. Then she sent him off to borrow some from her sister in the next village. She knew it would take him hours to walk there and back.

As soon as the door banged shut, Baila made a sign and hung it in the window.

BAILA'S CAFE

Luscious Latkes

One Kopek Each

She took down the magic frying pan. Of course, she remembered Moishe's words about the stranger's warning: "To Moishe this gift was given, and *only Moishe must use it.*" But why shouldn't the magic work for her too? After all, she was his wife.

Baila placed the pan over the fire. There was the sizzling sound! It grew louder and louder as she waited for the perfume of frying latkes to reach her nose. But instead a burning odor filled the kitchen. Baila pushed the pan away from the flame, but the smell grew stronger, catching in her throat. A plume of smoke uncoiled like a gray serpent. Dipping up some water, Baila flung it into the pan.

HISSSSS! The water splattered everywhere. And before she could blink, each droplet changed into a hairy little demon with pointy ears and a forked tail. The creatures danced around and around Baila, giggling and pelting her with burnt latkes. Then, climbing onto the chairs and the table, they shook empty handkerchiefs in her face. Baila spun this way and that until she was dizzy, but she could not escape them.

Just as she swooned to the floor, the door opened. In blew Moishe, on a cold draft. He was followed by Wishniak's own rabbi, and his wife, the *rebbitsin* whom Moishe had chanced to meet on his way out of town. It was the *rebbitsin* who sold candles to the villagers, and she had kindly given Moishe enough candles to last for the rest of the holiday. Moishe in turn had invited the couple home for latkes.

The demons took one look at the rabbi, shrieked in terror, jumped back into the pan, and vanished instantly in a belch of smoke. Baila was brought back to her senses by a whiff of the *rebbitsin's* smelling salts. For the first time in her life, she had nothing to say—the demons had scared her speechless!

Forever grateful to Moishe for saving her, Baila took time from her housework to help with the milking. She fed the cows and cleaned the shed. With his newfound love of cooking and entertaining, Moishe prepared meals and cared for the house. By the end of Hanukkah, Baila found that she could speak again, in a voice so kind that even the cows conversed with her. From then on, Moishe and Baila were seen delivering the milk together.

As for the magic frying pan, even back in Moishe's hands it refused to make another pancake. So instead of sitting on top of the wardrobe, it was sealed in a display case in the rabbi's courtyard. But the fame of its latkes and the tale of its demons spread, and soon folks were traveling from far and wide to see it. Everyone hoped to see the "demons under glass" making a surprise appearance. (And sometimes they did!)

The visitors to Wishniak needed food and lodging, heels for their boots, and hay for their horses. Soon the village grew into a bustling market town where no one went hungry. And for years to come, even on the coldest Hanukkah night, candles burned brightly in the windows and the smell of frying latkes rose over the houses in a golden haze that seemed to reach the stars.

Snow on the rooftops
Milk in the pail
That is the end
Of this Hanukkah tale!

H A N U K K A H

Hanukkah is a Jewish winter festival celebrating the victory of the Maccabees over the Syrians in 167 B.C. The Syrian ruler, Antiochus IV, worshipped Greek gods and wanted to force the Jews to do the same. He had a huge statue of Zeus placed in the great Temple in Jerusalem, the most holy place of Jewish worship. Judah Maccabee led a small band of fighters against the strong army of Antiochus for three years. Although the Jewish rebels had little training and their equipment was poor, they triumphed. But the Syrians had sacked and burned the Temple. The Jews immediately began to rebuild it. According to legend, when Judah Maccabee lit the lamps of the great candelabrum, called a menorah, there was oil enough to burn for only one day, yet miraculously the oil burned for eight days and nights.

Jewish people traditionally light candles in their homes for eight nights during the festival of Hanukkah. Starting with one the first evening, a light is added each night to one of eight holders on a family's menorah. The shammes, a ninth candle often standing apart from or taller than the rest, is used to light the others.

A GLOSSARY

dreidel (dray-dul):
A four-sided top children play with during Hanukkah,
in a special game to win candy or small coins

knippel (k'nip-pul):
A knot in a handkerchief, used as a purse

latkes (lot-kas or lot-kees):
Potato pancakes fried in oil, traditionally eaten during Hanukkah

menorah (meh-nor-ah; rhymes with aurora):
An eight-branched candelabrum lit on the eight nights of Hanukkah

meshugah (mi-shu-gah, with the u sounded like that in sugar):
Crazy

rebbitsin (reh-bit-zun):
A rabbi's wife

schlemiel (shluh-meel):
A foolish or clumsy person, or a pip-squeak

shammes (sha-mis; rhymes with promise):
The ninth candle on the Hanukkah menorah, used to light the others

To my father, Morris Krauss, the Moishe in my life, and to my friend
Bonnie Abrams Travieso, who named this story —L. K. M.

To my dad, Donn P. Slonim —D. S.

First Chronicle Books edition published in 2005.

Text © 2000 by Laura Krauss Melmed.
Illustrations © 2000 by David Slonim.
Originally published by HarperCollins Publishers in 2000.
All rights reserved.
Manufactured in China.

Library of Congress Cataloging-in-Publication Data
Melmed, Laura Krauss.
  Moishe's miracle : a Hanukkah story / by Laura Krauss Melmed ; illustrated by David Slonim.—1st Chronicle Books ed.
     p. cm.
  Summary: Moishe, a milkman who is kind to everyone in his poor village of Wishniak, receives a magic frying pan that produces an
unlimited supply of delicious Hanukkah latkes.
  ISBN 0-8118-5233-4 (library edition) — ISBN 0-8118-5234-2 (pbk.)
  [1. Fairy tales. 2. Hanukkah—Fiction. 3. Magic—Fiction. 4. Jews—Fiction.] I. Slonim, David, ill. II. Title.
  PZ8+
  [E]—dc22
  2005013292

Distributed in Canada by Raincoast Books, 9050 Shaughnessy Street, Vancouver, British Columbia V6P 6E5

10 9 8 7 6 5 4 3 2

Chronicle Books LLC, 85 Second Street, San Francisco, California 94105

www.chroniclekids.com